AF407599

the simple
Fast
Weight Loss

Weight reduction is perhaps the most sultry theme ever. Everybody is by all accounts attempting to get thinner these days. Most eating regimen programs are about weight reduction and body weight is regularly utilized as a pointer of wellness progress. Be that as it may, this is a wrong methodology.

Your definitive objective ought to consistently be to lose fat and decreasing abundance muscle to fat ratio is the thing that you ought to be worried about. Weight reduction and Fat misfortune isn't something very similar! Numerous individuals befuddle the two terms, regularly accepting that they mean the equivalent, when in truth weight reduction and fat misfortune are totally different from each other. This article will assist you with seeing how weight reduction is unique in relation to fat misfortune and how fat misfortune is far better than weight reduction in practically all manners.

What Is Weight Loss? (Weight reduction = Muscle Loss + Fat Loss + Water Loss)

Weight reduction is endeavoring to bring down your absolute body weight. It just alludes to a lower number on a scale.

Your body weight is made out of the considerable number of parts of your body, for example, muscles, fat, bones, water, organs, tissues, blood, water and so forth..

At the point when you get in shape, you lose a tad of... fat, muscle and water.

You lose fat however almost no and alongside the fat you lose muscle and some measure of water. The higher you lessen your calorie admission, the quicker you drop weight and the more bulk you lose.

Do realize your muscle matters? Loss of muscle influences your wellbeing and your general appearance

At the point when you get thinner too rapidly, your body can't keep up its muscle. Since muscle requires more calories to continue itself, your body starts to process it with the goal that it can hold the approaching calories for its endurance. It secures it fat stores as a guard system to guarantee your endurance if there should arise an occurrence of future starvation and rather utilize fit tissue or muscle to give it calories it needs to keep its fundamental organs, for example, your cerebrum, heart, kidneys and liver working. In the event that you arrive at a point where you have next to no fat or muscle, your body will process your organs to keep your mind working prompting respiratory failure, stroke and liver and kidney disappointment.

As the body loses more bulk, the body's general metabolic rate diminishes. The metabolic rate is the rate at which the body consumes calories and is somewhat dictated by the measure of muscle you have.

So the more muscle you have, the higher your metabolic rate; the less muscle you have, the lower your metabolic rate and less calories you consume. This clarifies why it is pivotal to secure your metabolic rate and not have muscle misfortune.

Loss of muscle likewise prompts loss of tone underneath the skin leaving you delicate and misshapen with no structure or shape. On the off chance that you get more fit too quickly, your skin won't have the opportunity to modify either. Likewise muscle is the thing that invigorates you and loss of it implies a frail body.

With weight reduction you shrivel and turn into a littler variant of yourself with a delicate casing with droopy skin.

Weight reduction works in the short hurry to make you littler yet is brief, nearly everybody bounce back and recovers the weight. This powers you to discover another eating routine. And afterward another, and another - on the grounds that in the end they'll all come up short.

What Is Fat Loss?

(Fat Loss = Loss Of Stored Body Fat)

Fat misfortune is endeavoring to bring down your all out muscle versus fat - for example the level of your complete body weight that is comprised of fat.

The correct methodology for fat misfortune is to practice adroitly and eat wisely in a manner that keeps up muscle and spotlights on fat misfortune solely.

The muscle you have isn't there until the end of time.

On the off chance that you don't take care of it and don't utilize it - you lose it. An appropriate arrangement with right blend of obstruction and cardiovascular preparing with satisfactory movement and a correct nourishment intend to help it can assist you with accomplishing this. Exercise just lifts the consuming procedure however doesn't simply liquefy the fat away all alone - on the off chance that you don't make a shortage and feed the body excessively
it won't contact the put away fuel holds. On the hand in the event that you radically cut your calories and don't take care of your muscle appropriately or don't exercise and utilize your muscle, you will lose it. Fat misfortune is tied in with finding that correct equalization.

With fat misfortune you keep up the muscle and keep the metabolic rate running high.

You additionally create more grounded connective tissue, more tight skin and more grounded bones and joints. With fat misfortune you change your body.

Fat misfortune is a way of life approach where you give your body what it needs without denying and stunning it with danger of starvation. You get the opportunity to see moderate yet changeless consistent advancement.
It might sound odd, yet it's conceivable to get more slender without really observing an adjustment in your weight. This happens when you lose muscle versus fat while picking up muscle. Your weight remains the equivalent, even as you lose inches.

Lets perceive how this occurs.

Fat tissue is free and not thick. It consumes a ton of room in your body. Though muscle is progressively thick and occupies less room. At the point when you lose fat, this space is liberated and you can see inch misfortune. On the off chance that you are following a reliable quality preparing program, at that point gain in slender muscle tissue will adjust this loss of fat and weight remains the equivalent. Since muscle takes less space than fat, you lose inches and begin to look increasingly conditioned, slender and shapely.
steady quality preparing program at that point gain in slender muscle tissue will adjust this loss of fat and weight remains the equivalent. Since muscle takes less space than fat, you lose inches and begin to look increasingly conditioned, slender and shapely.

Legend: "Getting fit" signifies "Shedding pounds.

There are numerous normal weight reduction legends that individuals live by with regards to their wellbeing. It is troublesome on occasion to isolate the weight reduction fantasies and actuality based on what is valid. Many sound valid while others are simply ludicrous. I once read some place that on the off chance that you drink water around evening time that you are going to put on weight or that on the off chance that you scratch your head time after time you will lose your hair....

Weight reduction Myth # 1
The more weight that I need to lose the more exceptional my activity routine ought to be
Weight reduction Truth: Although having an exceptional exercise routine is extraordinary, there are a couple of things you ought to consider: the first being that everybody is at an alternate level with regards

to their wellness and how much power they can really deal with. In the event that you have been truly idle for various years, an exceptional work out for you may be, strolling a large portion of a mile daily. After you walk that half mile you notice that you are sweating profusely and that you are worn out. Nonetheless, for somebody who has been genuinely dynamic for a long time, strolling a large portion of a mile should be possible without a perspiration. Everybody has an alternate meaning of what "exceptional" is.

On the off chance that extraordinary for you is working out for an hour daily, however because of life's bustling timetable you just possess energy for 20 minutes every day, at that point those 20 minutes will go a very long way. It may not really be named "extreme", as per your definition, yet those little cardio minutes will have positive wellbeing modifying impacts. Fat Loss Myth # 2

Stress and weight gain don't go inseparably

Weight reduction Fact: This is one of those "ludicrous" fantasies. To learn all the more how stress is including lbs. to your life please download my free E-Book, "Brain science of Releasing Weight"

Weight reduction Myth # 3

I can get more fit while eating anything I desire
Weight reduction Truth: Sir Isaac Newton once said " What goes up must descend." There are characteristic rules that administer our lives. On the off chance that you hurl a ball noticeable all around, it will return.

You can sit on your sofa and envision and imagine that the ball will remaining above water noticeable all around, however common standards instruct us that it will descend. Same goes with regards to our weight.

This is one of the most widely recognized weight reduction legends out there. It is strange to imagine that your wellbeing and weight will be in balance if your nourishment comprises basically of twinkies, chips, and doughnuts. Sure you can copy it off by working out, however a great many people whose diet comprises of for the most part lousy nourishment are likely not restrained enough to adhere to an exercise schedule.

I do know a couple of individuals who, all things considered, appear as though they are fit as a fiddle, since they are not "fat, yet who have elevated cholesterol.

Because I feel frustrated about squashing the hearts of such a significant number of twinkie darlings out there, I would state this. You can eat low quality nourishment, treats, chips, dessert, pizza, burgers.... Those "spirit fulfilling nourishments", yet it ought to be with some restraint. Anything in overabundance is rarely acceptable.
Fat Loss Myth # 4

Skipping dinners is a decent method to shed pounds

Weight reduction Fact: There are various investigations that show that individuals who skip breakfast and eat less occasions during the day will in general be significantly heavier than who have a sound dietary breakfast and afterward eat 4-6 little dinners during the day.

The motivation to this may be the way that they get hungrier later on in the day, and might tend to over eat during different suppers of the day.

Weight reduction Myth # 5

I won't shed pounds while eating around evening time
Weight reduction Truth: You can over enjoy food during the day and not eat a solitary thing around evening time and you WILL put on weight. Just like the way that you can starve yourself during the day and eat throughout the night you despite everything will put on weight. The key here is balance. On the off chance that your body is revealing to you that it is eager, at that point maybe you ought to hear it out. In all actuality, over eating, while not working out, will make you put on weight; regardless of what time that you eat.

At whatever point I am ravenous around evening time, just like my propensity with different suppers during the day, I attempt to choose something that is normal in nature. Something like natural products, vegetables, or I may even make myself an organic product smoothie. During those minutes that I am longing for dessert or something sweet, I permit myself to get a few, and DO NOT feel remorseful about it. Numerous individuals who are overweight carry on with their life in blame and disgrace. I permit myself to get a few, notwithstanding, WITH MODERATION. Fat Loss Myth # 6

I'm not worthy until I shed pounds

Weight reduction Fact: The individual who doesn't feel worthy since they are fat is on the grounds that they are not adequate to themselves first.

The way that you think others see you depends on your perspective on yourself. I genuinely accept that one must turn out to be sincerely fit before getting truly fit. I have experienced these self-constraining feelings previously. When I understood that I was ALREADY ENOUGH according to God and that I had no compelling reason to substantiate myself to anybody or to get outside approval for my self-esteem, that had a significant effect for me. When you acknowledge yourself as what your identity is RIGHT NOW and understand that you are as of now enough according to God, you won't feel like you are not adequate in light of your weight.

Weight reduction Myth # 7

I have to slice calories to get thinner quicker

Weight reduction Truth: Cutting your calories down may be an incredible thing, in the event that you are radically gorging and stuffing your face. Be that as it may, in the event that you are eating relatively, at that point cutting calories may have an aversive effect. On the off chance that you are cutting calories and are starving your body, at that point that will bring down your digestion, or at the end of the day back it off, which may bring about you really not losing any weight whatsoever, regardless of whether you are "cutting calories"

Fat Loss Myth # 8
Skipping dinners will assist me with getting more fit

Weight reduction Fact: Skipping suppers may really make you put on weight! You will turn out to be excessively eager and will inevitably need to eat.

This will thump your digestion off course and will in the end back it off. Think about a vehicle coming up short on gas (food), in the event that you don't top it off, it will in the long run quit working. Same goes for our body, we have to keep it filled continually.

Weight reduction Myth # 9

I think I have hereditary weight gain, it runs in my family!

Weight reduction Truth: Can somebody say E-X-C-U-S-E-S? I won't deny that there may be propensities for substantial guardians to bring up overwhelming kids who will stay overwhelming their entire lives, yet I don't accept that there is really a "fat" quality or DNA out there. What we do acquire from our family, essentially the individuals who legitimately raised us, are our perspectives and convictions.

Your perspectives about food, cash, religion, governmental issues, instruction, and so on depend on how you were raised. In the event that you were brought up in a home where the essential dinners prepared where seared nourishments, at that point you may tend to keep cooking and eating singed food sources for a mind-blowing duration. On the off chance that that is the situation, at that point you may be somewhat overwhelming around the midriff. The simple activity is at fault it on the individuals who were responsible for your childhood, in any case, you ALWAYS have a decision to change.

Fat Loss Myth # 10
Eating well is excessively hard

Weight reduction Fact: Eating well is the most straightforward thing in the world.....once you have prepared yourself to do it. How often have you put an objective to get more fit or to "eat better"? The initial barely any days you are doing extraordinary, eating a wide range of nourishments which you regularly wouldn't eat. At that point something interesting began to occur, you returned to your old propensities and practices. This has transpired in different regions outside of your wellbeing.

It could be with bringing in cash, searching for a new position, or in your connections. Making another propensity requires some investment on the grounds that our cerebrum's don't care for change. Change to the mind is risky. In any case, in the event that you might want to get familiar with how our mind endeavors to disrupt us from making new propensities at that point please download my free E-book, "Brain research of Releasing Weight"

Weight reduction Myth # 11

You need to surrender your preferred nourishments to get thinner

Weight reduction Truth: What might a world without chocolate and without pepperoni pizza resemble??? I figure it would be an agonizing world to live in!! lol, presently on a genuine note I totally can't help contradicting this fantasy. You are unquestionably ready to eat your preferred nourishments. Denying yourself of this sort of joy isn't fun, and honestly you likely WILL eat it at any rate.
As has been referenced previously, the genuine key is control. In the event that you are a steak darling, at that point maybe it probably won't be the best things to eat it each and every day, except maybe on more than one occasion per week.

The individuals who realize me by and by realize that I LOVE chicken wings with pizza.
Ideally where I wouldn't put on any weight and my veins were stop up less, I couldn't imagine anything
better than to eat it a few times each week, well increasingly like each day. In any case, I realize that those aren't the most beneficial of food decisions so I have it around 2-3 times each month. I am not surrendering my preferred nourishments, I am simply eating it with some restraint so it doesn't make up for lost time to me as overabundance weight.

Fat Loss Myth # 12

Gorging is brought about by hunger

Weight reduction Fact: Nice attempt there. In the event that no one but we could fault "hunger" for it.

Actually, this individual we call hunger has nothing to do with you OVEREATING. It may have something to do your body disclosing to you that the time has come to "fuel up" and that it needs food, however that isn't a sign that one ought to indulge. What makes numerous individuals gorge are various reasons. One of the primary ones is feeling of pressure, gloom, depression, uneasiness, dread, and other downsizing feelings of that nature.

Ordinarily food can be a methods for fulfilling your necessities. You may be really getting your requirements met through your nourishments. For instance, in the event that you carry on with a forlorn life, and aren't extremely cheerful, at that point food could maybe be a methods for you feeling upbeat and console. There are different articles that I have composed regarding this matter yet do the trick it

The most ideal approach to get more fit isn't to crash slim down or have explosions of activity, however to roll out moderate improvements. The most ideal approach to roll out these improvements and stick to them is to make a get-healthy plan. This can be utilized to set out your objectives, how you will accomplish them, and changes as they happen.

So as to get more fit you have to asses your vitality admission. Food is utilized as vitality for your body, and any vitality not utilized is put away as fat. It is thusly basic that you just take in the vitality you need and increment your movement level so as to shed pounds. When lessening your calorie admission, it is fundamental that you make changes that you are probably going to adhere to as crash diets may prompt 'yo-yo' abstaining from excessive food intake.

Eating around 300-500 calories less every week will prompt a weight reduction of 1-2lbs per week, while it isn't a lot of week by week it signifies around 52lbs every year. It is likewise significant not to skip suppers as this would make you overcompensate later in the day and nibble more.

Expanding action levels should be possible effectively for instance attempting to complete 20 minutes of strolling a day, for example, strolling short excursions than utilizing the vehicle. By discovering something that you appreciate you are bound to adhere to it.

By utilizing a get-healthy plan you can execute these progressions and stick to them. It might likewise work best on the off chance that you record your arrangement, keeping a note of your objectives, changes in weight and accomplishments to assist you with keeping on target.

While you may not perceive any quick changes, stay with it. Try not to let any weight gain put you off, and rather take a gander at your program and check whether anything needs to change, for example, expanding your movement levels. Furthermore, when you arrive at your objectives celebrate by regarding yourself to something, for example, a night out or another outfit to make your weight reduction much better.

Another part of your health improvement plan could be a food journal. By recording all the food and drink you take in during the week you will think that its simpler to see where you are turning out badly. You can survey the journal toward the finish of every week to get a more clear image of exactly how much calories you truly are expending.

In the event that your eating routine

looks sound but then you despite everything aren't losing any weight, you could need to take a gander at your segment sizes to ensure you are essentially not eating excessively.

Any progressions that you do cause will to be best whenever presented steadily. This will imply that you are bound to adhere to them, which means you can present more without feeling under an excessive amount of tension. Simple changes to make incorporate; trading white bread for earthy colored bread, full fat milk for half fat milk, removing snacks and so on. You ought to likewise pick a health improvement plan that supports steady weight reduction as opposed to quick weight reduction. By doing this, the weight you lose is bound to remain off and, by setting attainable month to month targets as opposed to ridiculous week after week targets, you are bound to meet them. While picking a health improvement plan it is significant that you pick one that is directly for you. The most significant factor to consider is your wellbeing, so don't pick an arrangement that has silly cases and could conceivable be dangerous. Set reachable objectives and make changes that you are probably going to adhere to for a mind-blowing remainder, keeping the weight off for good.The most ideal approach to get thinner isn't to crash consume less calories or have explosions of activity, however to roll out moderate improvements. The most ideal approach to roll out these improvements and stick to them is to make a health improvement plan.

This can be utilized to set out your objectives, how you will accomplish them, and changes as they happen.

So as to get in shape you have to asses your vitality admission. Food is utilized as vitality for your body, and any vitality not utilized is put away as fat. It is consequently basic that you just take in the vitality you need and increment your movement level so as to get more fit. When decreasing your calorie consumption, it is basic that you make changes that you are probably going to adhere to as crash diets may prompt 'yo-yo' eating less junk food. Eating around 300-500 calories less every week will prompt a weight reduction of 1-2lbs per week, while it isn't a lot of week after week it means around 52lbs every year. It is likewise significant not to skip suppers as this would make you overcompensate later in the day and nibble more. Expanding movement levels should be possible effectively for instance attempting to complete 20 minutes of strolling a day, for example, strolling short excursions than utilizing the vehicle. By discovering something that you appreciate you are bound to adhere to it.

By utilizing a health improvement plan you can actualize these progressions and stick to them. It might likewise work best on the off chance that you record your arrangement, keeping a note of your objectives, changes in weight and accomplishments to assist you with keeping on target. While you may not perceive any prompt changes, stay with it. Try not to let any weight gain put you off, and rather take a gander at your program and check whether anything needs to

change, for example, expanding your action levels. Furthermore, when you arrive at your
objectives celebrate by regarding yourself to something, for example, a night out or another outfit to make your weight reduction considerably better.

Another part of your health improvement plan could be a food journal. By recording all the food and drink you take in during the week you will think that its simpler to see where you are turning out badly. You can audit the journal toward the finish of every week to get a more clear image of exactly how much calories you truly are devouring.
 In the event that your eating regimen looks solid but then you despite everything aren't losing any weight, you could need to take a gander at your bit sizes to ensure you are basically not eating excessively.

Any progressions that you do cause will to be best whenever presented step by step. This will imply that you are bound to adhere to them, which means you can present more without feeling under an excessive amount of tension. Simple changes to make incorporate; trading white bread for earthy colored bread, full fat milk for half fat milk, removing snacks and so forth. You ought to likewise pick a health improvement plan that supports continuous weight reduction instead of quick weight reduction. By doing this, the weight you lose is bound to remain off and, by setting feasible month to month targets as opposed to ridiculous week after week targets, you are bound to meet them.

While picking a health improvement plan it is significant that you pick one that is directly for you.

The most significant factor to consider is your wellbeing, so don't pick an arrangement that has ridiculous cases and could conceivable be unsafe. Set reachable objectives and make changes that you are probably going to adhere to for an incredible remainder, keeping the weight off for good.

It's entirely astounding what we in America will never really weight. It's additionally quite intriguing to me that with all the manners in which that we need to shed those undesirable pounds, that we as a Nation, are more overweight than any other time in recent memory.

That is fascinating without a doubt. There is by all accounts a type of association between the systems that we use to shed pounds and our capacity to really lose weight...and to really keep it off.

There are a bigger number of diets plans and projects than we realize how to manage, and increasingly nourishing items and supper plans for advancing a slimmer you, yet shouldn't something be said about exercise? It's getting evident to me that significantly after so long of research that unmistakably shows that activity is a basic segment to effective and enduring weight reduction, numerous in the public eye are as yet searching for ways (and it appears any path conceivable) to stay away from it.

With the entirety of the yo-yo diets and starvation eats less, alongside the other wacky dietary projects intended to "blow-burn" your fat and drop the weight right away, numerous individuals have started to embrace a "present time and place" approach which has advanced eagerness, disappointment, and in the end disappointment. For some individuals, after some time this way to deal with weight reduction has created a battered and wounded digestion in urgent need of a makeover so as to start working at an elevated level by and by. With a digestion in such an undermined state, it bodes well to give it all the assist it with canning get. On the off chance that you can identify with any of what I've quite recently composed, at that point I would energetically compliment a sound exercise normal as a potential answer for the individuals who have opposed to this point. It might really end up being your best answer for more viable weight reduction than you've encountered with diet alone.

How Quick Weight Loss Programs Can Sabotage Your Weight Loss

The difficult that I've found with the brisk weight reduction eats less and the low-calorie "starvation" consumes less calories is that they don't advance safe weight reduction. Commonly, when pounds drop off a lot of it is water from slender muscle tissue, and almost no of it is really what you truly need to come off...and that is fat. That, however during the time spent losing the entirety of this weight, we are likewise affecting our digestion by not taking in the necessary measure of calories, and when this doesn't occur, our digestion really plunges. That causes us less ready to consume the same number of calories as we did preceding starting the eating routine. I don't think about you, yet that is NOT what I need happening when I'm attempting to get in shape. So what occurs, is the transitory delight that goes with the weight reduction, at that point the dissatisfaction as the pounds begin to crawl back until, in the long run, we end up where we began (if not heavier).

Why Diet Alone May Not Provide the Weight Loss Results You Desire

As I referenced before in this article, numerous individuals endeavor weight reduction through dietary alteration way of life change without exploiting exercise as a successful instrument in helping themselves arrive at their weight reduction objective. In any event, when nourishment is sound, and the weight decrease plan is reasonable, there is as yet a significant issue which numerous individuals either neglect to acknowledge or only level out deny (no doubt because of their scorn for work out), and that is the matter of the every day calorie shortfall that activity can make past that of simply diet alone. The common exercise meeting can consume somewhere in the range of 100 to 500 calories, and on the off chance that you factor those calories with those not expended through the day by day diet, there could be a shortage far more noteworthy than through eating regimen alone. On the off chance that 250 calories were consumed exercise, and there was a decrease in calorie admission of 250 that equivalent day, that makes for a complete decrease of 500 calories for that day. At the point when accomplished for an entire week, that would prompt lost one pound.

That may not appear a lot, yet who wouldn't have any desire to shed 4 pounds in a month and have it remain off? This isn't to make reference to the way that a similar recipe could be applied each month from there on. I trust you're ready to see the conceivable outcomes. Finally, for the individuals who may favor the "no activity" approach, consider that when exercise is a customary piece of your program, you'll have the option to eat more and not need to stress as a lot over putting on weight. That sounds extraordinary to me. Sign me up!

Step by step instructions to Jump-Start Your Metabolism So You Can Experience More Effective Weight Loss

Increasingly compelling weight reduction ordinarily results when quality nourishment and weight the board techniques are joined with a sound exercise program. As a snappy suggestion which I truly trust you follow, avoid the speedy weight reduction counts calories. They are a catastrophe waiting to happen. As an approach to do this current, it's significant that you think about your weight reduction as a procedure that will proceed for whatever length of time that you are alive. Such a large number of individuals need snappy outcomes, yet neglect to think about the long haul. That will most likely prompt disappointment, debilitation, and inevitably, disappointment. As another significant suggestion, center around improving your nourishment gradually...over time. Such a large number of calorie counters have embraced the "Without any weaning period" way to deal with their nourishment which works perhaps marginally better than stopping smoking immediately.

One most basic suggestion that I accept will be without a doubt the KEY to kicking off your digestion and delivering progressively powerful weight reduction is to quickly join.

customary exercise into your week by week schedule. Does it should be ordinary? In no way, shape or form! You can see extraordinary outcomes with only 2-3 days out of every week, and astonishing outcomes with more days of the week. Ensure that your routine incorporates cardiovascular activities, for example, strolling, cycling, swimming, or different exercises that you appreciate. As critically, be certain that there is some type of obstruction preparing in your everyday practice. Activities, for example, push-ups, pull-ups, high-intensity aerobics, and exercises do some incredible things for kicking off your digestion and giving you the outcomes that you've generally longed for. In conclusion, consistency is foremost. No good thing occurs with inconsistent and dreary exertion. Make certain to put forth a strong effort and you will receive the incredible benefit of effective weight reduction that endures forever Weight loss is a topic discussed by more than 90% of people in the world, people looking for fast and effective ways to lose weight. Many try to find the right weight loss center to have the ultimate weight loss control.

The most common method people use is diet pills, but there has been talk that diet pills don't really work, they work if you are taking them and once you stop the pounds return. This happens when one only realize on diet pills to accomplish their goal. I want to help you understand the benefits of using a good diet pill and give you a way to keep off the pounds.

Firstly what is good weight loss?

Good weight loss is the loss of body mass in an effort to improve once fitness, appearance and health.

 This is the main reasons why people search for ways to lose weight. There are so many products out there that offer fast weight loss, the question is do they really work as good as they say? Yes some do the problem with most people is that they don't look at the reasons why they have the extra weight that they are trying to get rid of. The first step in weight loss is to educate yourself about yourself, know your body and your mind. These are a few things for you to think about before you start your weight loss journey.

1.   How much weight do you need to loss?

2.   Why do you need to loss that amount of weight?

3.   Have you tried to loss weight before?

4.   If yes, think about what could have went wrong

5.   Do you want a quick fix or a life long fix?
6.   Do you eat healthy meals?

7.   Do you exercise or do any physical activities?

These questions form the foundation to you reaching your weight loss goal, let me explain.

1. Knowing how much weight you need to loss and why you need to loss it gives you a goal.

2. If you have tried losing the weight before and it never work then there might be some thing you missing out.

3. The quick fix or life long fix is the commitment you are willing to put into losing the unwanted weight.

4. The healthy eating and exercise, well if you eat healthy meals and exercise every day and you still don't loss weight then it might be a medical condition. When it comes to using diet pills for losing weight you need to plan a program and a life style change to help you accomplish your goals. Your desired weight loss goal should remain constantly in your mind. Make a good weight loss start, lose the weight and control your body. Diet pills help you loss the unwanted weight quickly and the planning process helps you keep off the weight lost when you stop taking the diet pills. Nobody wants to take pills for the rest of their life. Weight loss

comes down to reducing extra calories from food and beverages and increasing calories burned through physical activity. The key is to commit to a healthy diet (increase fruit and vegetable intake) and a good daily exercise plan. Planning your daily meals and physical activity are the best ways to keep your calories in control and before you know, it will be a way of life and you won't need to plan every meal and activity it will be a normal part of your day just like reading a book or watching television.

For those that have a sweet tooth there are a wide range of dieting snacks full of flavor for you to try but remember although they are for dieters you still need to control yourself so don't over do it. You can fit in a measured snack into your daily meal plan.

Never forget the main source: The key to successful weight loss is a commitment to making permanent changes in your diet and exercise habits. The experience of reaching your goals is priceless and exciting. Enjoy you're your program and remember your goal.

Weight reduction is a basic issue in the present society with stoutness on the ascent and individuals at last acknowledging what being overweight is doing to their bodies, their wellbeing and inevitably their ways of life.

Weight reduction is useful for some conditions. It is of genuine advantage in diabetes, hypertension, brevity of breath, joint issues and raised cholesterol.

Weight reduction is conceivable with practice and solid suppers alone, yet including great quality protein and building slender bulk will assist you with losing all the more rapidly, helping you to keep the weight off and remain sound.

Weight reduction is for all intents and purposes ensured in the event that one adheres to the guidelines of the eating routine.
Weight reduction rudiments: eat a bigger number of calories than you use and you'll gain weight; utilize more than you eat and you'll lose it. Weight reduction is presently an objective which can be reached actually effectively on the off chance that we adhere to a preparation system, diet plan. In any case, for a few, medical procedure might be the main expectation.

Careful procedures have advanced in the course of recent decades, and most are powerful, as in they do normally prompt generous weight reduction.

Be that as it may, all specialists do concur that the most ideal approach to keep up weight reduction is to follow a sound way of life. Whichever approach you like, the way to long haul achievement is a moderate consistent weight reduction. It is demonstrated that it is critical to set yourself up intellectually for your weight reduction venture and the way of life transforms you are going to experience.

For people who are extremely chubby, medical procedure to sidestep parts of the stomach and small digestive system may on occasion be the main compelling methods for creating continued and critical weight reduction.

The essential factor in accomplishing and keeping up weight reduction is a deep rooted pledge to ordinary exercise and reasonable dietary patterns. You will locate that all degrees of your life are improved with weight reduction which brings you so much close to home fulfillment.

On the off chance that dietary patterns are not totally and forever changed, the weight reduction gave by an eating routine won't keep going long. In the event that you experience the ill effects of, or figure you may experience the ill effects of, an ailment you ought to counsel your primary care physician before beginning a weight reduction and/or practice system.

Drinking water is one of the most fast weight reduction tips that dieticians propose to individuals and prompts 100+ calories extra consumed a day. Each twenty sodas you skip from your ordinary admission likens to around one pound of weight reduction.

Fasting: While fasting has a significant impact in certain eating regimens, it is for the most part not suggested for safe weight reduction.

Diet

Dietitians are nutritionists who work straightforwardly with customers or patients in regards to their dietary needs. Slimming down decreases your caloric admission however practicing causes you consume more calories. DIET Weight misfortune is indispensable if stoutness is available. Eating fewer carbs is simpler than you at any point envisioned. On a vegan diet, weight reduction should be an issue.

An even diminished calorie diet containing moderate fat is suggested. The consideration of various types of organic products into weight reduction eats less is a solid method of managing starvation, just as giving the body those supplements and nutrients it needs to work appropriately.
Exercise While You Diet: Weight misfortune is tied in with lessening your caloric admission while you increment the calories you consume. Most importantly choose how much weight you need to lose, and set yourself a reasonable objective, in a perfect world with the assistance of your dietitian or specialist.

An eating regimen that works for certain individuals doesn't work for other people. A solid breakfast is one of the key components of a sound eating routine and considerable weight reduction. Most trend abstains from food, whenever followed intently, will bring about weight reduction because of caloric limitation.

Additionally, calorie counters who neglect to embrace better exercise and dietary patterns will recover the shed pounds and perhaps more. As it starts, a lot of water will be shed, driving the health food nut to believe that noteworthy weight decrease is occurring.
Counsel your primary care physician, for any medical issue and before utilizing any enhancements, rolling out dietary improvements, or before rolling out any improvements in recommended prescriptions.

A significant part of the early weight reduction on a low calorie diet speaks to loss of muscle tissue as opposed to loss of fat.

The same number of as 85% of health food nuts who don't practice all the time recover their shed pounds inside two years. Over and again losing and recovering weight (yo-yo counting calories) urges the body to store fat and may expand a patient's danger of creating coronary illness.

Eating three adjusted, moderate-divide suppers daily with the primary feast at noontime is a more powerful approach to forestall stoutness than fasting or crash eats less carbs, which persuade the body that there is a continuous starvation. Present day medication has discovered approaches to broaden our life expectancy through dietary limitation.

For your wellbeing, consistently counsel your primary care physician before making any noteworthy dietary, healthful or way of life changes. The American Heart Association (AHA) for the most part suggests an eating regimen with under 30% fat. Person's way of life, food inclinations, readiness capacities, nibble propensities, longings, and so forth, should all be viewed as when building up a dietary arrangement. It is significant that the nourishment advisor tailor the eating regimen to the person instead of embracing a "one-size-fits-all" approach. After weight reduction, lower-fat eating regimens might be the best. For the vast majority, being overweight is an aftereffect of a deficient measure of activity, an insufficient way of life normal and an inadequately adjusted eating routine.

Most high-fiber nourishments are likewise high in water and low in calories, making them must-have diet food sources. Solvent fiber can assist with bringing down cholesterol; insoluble contains toxic filaments that add mass to our eating regimens.
A few specialists accept calorie counters have better control on the off chance that they eat a few scaled down suppers for the duration of the day. Exercise and a fair eating routine are the key factors in fat misfortune and weight decrease.

Drinking water is one of the most quick weight reduction tips that dieticians recommend to individuals and prompts 100+ calories extra consumed a day.

A definitive tip to possible achievement: customary exercise and a fair eating regimen. Add one cheat day to your eating routine to free yourself of desires.

Eat a sound eating routine loaded up with bunches of vegetables, natural products, and entire grain items.

Fasting: While fasting has a significant impact in certain eating regimens, it is by and large not suggested for safe weight reduction.
 Medical procedure

Be that as it may, for some in this circumstance, weight reduction medical procedure is the main expectation. Perhaps the soonest structure was gastric detour medical procedure.
There are numero

us types of medical procedure nowadays and all have advantages and disadvantages.

There are as yet generous dangers, be that as it may, similarly as with any significant medical procedure. For the individuals who accept medical procedure is the best alternative, talking with an accomplished doctor is basic.

For people who are beefy beyond belief, medical procedure to sidestep parts of the stomach and small digestive system may now and again be the main powerful methods for creating continued and huge weight reduction.
Such heftiness medical procedure, in any case, can be dangerous, and it is performed uniquely on patients for whom different systems have fizzled

and whose corpulence genuinely compromises wellbeing. On the off chance that break hernia side effects are constant and don't react to abstain from food and medicine, medical procedure may get fundamental.

Today, most specialists choose to perform laparoscopic medical procedure, since it is insignificantly obtrusive and recuperation time is decreased.

Consume

On the off chance that you envision yourself getting thinner and consuming calories during typical every day action, you will shed pounds and muscle versus fat. It cellularly affects the body, making fat cells discharge their put away fat to be copied as vitality. The food you eat during the day ought to be consumed action.

Exercise While You Diet: Weight misfortune is tied in with decreasing your caloric admission while you increment the calories you consume. Eating fewer carbs diminishes your caloric admission however practicing causes you consume more calories.

We as a whole realize that to accomplish a sound weight reduction we have to consume a larger number of calories than what we take in. Exercise expands the metabolic rate by making muscle, which consumes a greater number of calories than fat.
At the point when ordinary exercise is joined with steady, stimulating dinners, calories keep on consuming at a quickened rate for a few hours. Calories consumed relying upon your action level.

In addition to the fact that fat provides a feeling of totality, eating a sufficient solid fat called omega-3 unsaturated fats may make your digestion consume fat all the more effectively. On the off chance that your weight stays consistent, you are most likely taking in a similar measure of calories you consume every day.

In case you're gradually putting on weight after some time, all things considered, your caloric admission is more noteworthy than the quantity of calories you consume your day by day exercises.
The quantity of calories we consume every day is needy upon our basal metabolic rate (BMR), the quantity of calories we consume every hour just by being alive and keeping up body capacities and our degree of physical movement.

Our weight additionally assumes a job in deciding what number of calories we consume very still - more calories are required to keep up your body in its current express, the more prominent your body weight. Somebody whose activity includes substantial physical work will normally consume a bigger number of calories in a day than somebody who sits at a work area the majority of the day (a stationary activity).

For individuals who don't have employments that require exceptional physical movement, practice or expanded physical action can build the quantity of calories consumed.
To lose one pound, you should consume roughly 3500 calories well beyond what you as of now consume doing day by day exercises. Utilize a calorie mini-computer to make sense

of what number of calories you consume while sitting, standing, working out, lifting loads, and so on. In case you're eating less calories than you're consuming, you'll get thinner.

As it is notable when the body doesn't get enough calories it begins to consume the fat that was saved in the fat tissue.

Exercise will assist you with consuming abundance calories and fat, and will likewise assist with conditioning and assemble muscle. Holding muscle is the way to ideal fat consuming digestion Speedy weight reduction eats less carbs are well known because of the quicker beginning weight reduction they can accomplish and they are not so much hurtful but rather more useful. You get more fit quick during the underlying stages, because of the overal deficit of water weight since protein and sugars both assist hold with watering in body cells. Snappy weight reduction abstains from food are only a transitory arrangement and don't assist you with making perpetual changes to your dietary patterns.

Does this imply speedy weight reduction consumes less calories don't work? They do, yet just when you comprehend the job that fast weight reduction eats less carbs play in your general way of life. The significant thing before beginning any eating routine is to ask, "Would i be able to do this for an amazing remainder?" If the appropriate response is no, at that point don't attempt the eating regimen; it will possibly hurt you over the long haul in the event that you start a yo-yo pattern of weight "misfortune gain-misfortune" over and over.

Snappy weight reduction slims down are not planned for drawn out use. In spite of the fact that you may not see an issue from the outset, your body will before long quit reacting to the eating routine and the weight reduction will arrive at a level. Speedy weight reduction slims down, say proficient dermatologists, frequently need legitimate nourishment and fast weight reduction in itself can likewise trigger digestion changes that influence hair development. For the most advantageous hair, doctors state that the best get-healthy plans are decreased calorie eats less carbs that advance steady weight reduction and a sound eating regimen utilizing nourishments from all the nutrition types.

Snappy weight reduction slims down are not planned for drawn out use. In spite of the fact that you may not see an issue from the outset, your body will before long quit reacting to the eating routine and the weight reduction will arrive at a level. Speedy weight reduction slims down, say proficient dermatologists, frequently need legitimate nourishment and fast weight reduction in itself can likewise trigger digestion changes that influence hair development. For the most advantageous hair, doctors state that the best get-healthy plans are decreased calorie eats less carbs that advance steady weight reduction and a sound eating regimen utilizing nourishments from all the nutrition types.

Exercise and diet go connected at the hip with an effective weight reduction plan. Exercise ought to be agreeable, else you won't proceed. In the event that you believe you don't possess energy for anything, have a go at bouncing rope, or join your activity into something different you do, for instance, in the event that you work or live in a tall structure, use the stairwell all over.

 Practicing does you nothing but bad on the off chance that you simply go out and eat more when you are done

 Eating less junk food is the principal key to any genuinely effective weight reduction, particularly when you need to ensure that you get those pounds off, however that you keep them off, as well.

Exercise and diet go connected at the hip with an effective weight reduction plan. Exercise ought to be agreeable, else you won't proceed. In the event that you believe you don't possess energy for anything, have a go at bouncing rope, or join your activity into something different you do, for instance, in the event that you work or live in a tall structure, use the stairwell all over. Practicing does you nothing but bad on the off chance that you simply go out and eat more when you are done.

 Eating less junk food is the principal key to any genuinely effective weight reduction, particularly when you need to ensure that you get those pounds off, however that you keep them off, as well.

Brisk weight reduction eats less accomplish work, however they work surprisingly better joined with standard supported physical movement for forty-five minutes or more in any event five days every week. Recollect that it's imperative to check with your doctor on the off chance that you have a significant measure of weight to lose, on the off chance that you have any kind of wellbeing condition, or potentially you don't practice all the time or are inactive.

Having breakfast each day is in opposition to the regular example for the normal overweight individual who is attempting to count calories. At that point they get ravenous and devour a large portion of their calories late in the day. Eating right utilizing pre-arranged plans that consolidate nourishments that reinforce as opposed to debilitate and swell your framework is basic. Fruitful counting calories is tied in with being set up with appropriate amounts of solid food in all circumstances. Eat standard suppers 5 times each day yet very little. Endeavor to eat adjusted and sound dinners while as yet controlling your caloric admission. Along these lines you will be bound to keep up your weight reduction as opposed to recovering the pounds. Rather than high-fat items, lower fat choices are suggested. These weight control plans likewise for the most part incorporate such things as entire grain nourishments, a lot of water, low-fat proteins and that's just the beginning.

One tip to quickly chop down your calorie admission is by diminishing your ordinary food parcel into equal parts. By and large, the serving sizes you get in eateries and cheap food joints are more than what you need. By diminishing your part size, you despite everything get the chance to make the most of your typical nourishments and chop down your calorie consumption right away!

Speedy weight reduction abstains from food flourish, both on the web and locally in your city. While nearby health improvement plans are commonly more costly than online projects, the up close and personal help might be actually what you have to assist you with dropping the abundance weight.

Lasting way of life changes are the best way to stay at your objective weight once you arrive at it. Snappy weight reduction diets will assist you with getting more fit, simply make sure to do it right, the solid way.

How often have you attempted to get in shape just to lose the inspiration to do as such in a couple of days? Every one of those magazines guarantee they realize how to shed those pounds and each one of those prevailing fashion eats less are making you exhausted. For what reason don't they work? You inquire. Well there is a basic explanation behind that. This is on the grounds that you don't comprehend your body. Truly individuals, your body needs as much compassion as you do when it isn't feeling admirably. However, a great many people simply prefer to get moving on gigantic starvation diets and afterward starting to pig out three days after the fact! How would you imagine that causes your body to feel? Confounded, neglected, and disliked.

In any case, on the off chance that you are up for some new preparing, we have the ideal weight reduction answers for you. These are arrangements that will work and give you the outcomes that nobody has had the option to give. On the off chance that you can follow these basic weight reduction strategies, at that point we promise you will shed those pounds simpler than any time in recent memory. In any case, all we need from you is a touch of sympathy - not for us, however for your own delightful body. Take a profound inhale and unwind - When you are prepared to start, you can begin perusing further.

UNDERSTANDING YOUR BODY

We have said it previously and we are stating it once more, compelling weight reduction is tied in with understanding your body. At the point when you have to complete something from somebody, your initial step is consistently to get into their heads, so you can get a knowledge into discovering what they truly need and what triggers them to state yes. This is actually how you are going to start your weight reduction. Purchase realizing what your body needs and what triggers it to gorge.

A WORD ABOUT CALORIE COUNTING

A few people underline totally on checking calories, and different projects will request that you jettison it totally. We propose that you mull over it, however don't let it overpower you. Comprehending what nourishments have higher calories will help you towards your weight reduction objectives

Be that as it may, we will disclose to you how not to let it beat your eating routine to destroy it.

Powerful WEIGHT LOSS VS QUICK WEIGHT LOSS

With regards to weight reduction, brisk is never on a par with viable. Since speedy weight reduction will just shed pounds the vast majority of you will rapidly restore, and let's be honest, on the off chance that you truly are here attempting to figure out how to get more fit, at that point those trend counts calories most likely made you wiped out. That is old news, correct?

All things considered, the uplifting news is currently you can proceed onward.

THE 60 TIPS

Truly. At last, the genuine article on powerful weight reduction. They may appear to be somewhat out-there from the start yet they will work for you.

1. Disregard your weight reduction objective. Enough has been said about defining objectives and afterward wanting to accomplish them. Be that as it may, let me reveal to you something - on the off chance that you are here understanding this, at that point this objective setting has most likely failed to help you. This is on the grounds that when you set a weight reduction objective, it implies adhering to a specific everyday practice. Also, the greater part of us as of now have such a great amount of going on in our lives that it's occasionally difficult to work along that set everyday practice.

2. Why you should keep a practical methodology. At the point when you skirt the normal it causes you so discouraged you really to feel like you are this huge failure who can't do anything right. That doesn't help presently isn't that right? Obviously it doesn't! So the initial step to fruitful weight reduction - quit contemplating that discouraging goal!

3. Set a persuading future target. A large portion of us will fail to help an objective to shed exhausting 100 pounds, however we will murder to get a couple of those limited licensed lambskins in a single size less, or to get into those hot pants you purchased last Christmas and can't fit into any longer.

4. Get into those pants. Simply pause for a moment, and envision yourself in

those garments that are just about a size or two in contrast. Envision how extraordinary you look! That is the thing that your new 'objective' is.

5. Love yourself the manner in which you are. Nobody likes being called 'fat' and 'monstrous'. Your body doesn't either!

6. Treat your body well. You need to figure out how to quit rewarding it like an undesirable bit of product and start rewarding it the manner in which it has the right to be dealt with - at exactly that point will it treat you back a similar way.

7. Take a gander at the mirror. Truly, look and reason with your body that you currently live during a time of larger sizes.

8. Locate the correct garments. There are sufficient flawless garments out

there that can and will highlight your excellence and shroud your little rotund issues. That is to say, please, dislike you are the one and only one! In any case for what reason would individuals even make hefty size garments!

9. Get yourself an extraordinary new outfit. A great many people hold their looking for after they have lost the weight. That is absolutely silly. Venture out of those loose jeans and that incredible perspiration shirt and go get yourself a flawless arrangement of garments and truly go out in those new pair of garments.

10. New garments, new you. Those garments speak to your new life as somebody who comprehends their body and is en route to fruitful weight reduction.

11. At the point when you look great, you feel better. Misery is the genuine factor

behind most sorts of weight gain. To dispose of sorrow will be to dispose of overabundance weight.

12. Disposing of sorrow. You have to discover counterfeit approaches to oppose despondency and be en route to another you. Wear pleasant garments; put resources into some extraordinary looking shoes. Get a few makeup or hair items that work for you. The key to progress is in your own hands.

13. Water is your new closest companion. Water is the most basic beverage you should join for effective weight reduction. It will likewise give you incredible skin.

14. Water is the new tasteful. You have to quit regarding water as some second-grade drink which doesn't represent those sweet refreshments.

Consider water a shimmering, precious stone beverage that cools and spreads happiness inside your body.

15. Cut down on sweet beverages. Supplant with water however much as could reasonably be expected. Sweet beverages give you a dreadful skin, overabundance weight and malignant growth. Think about that before you taste out of that disturbing pop.

16. The downsides of sweet drinks. On the off chance that you are a normal American, at that point you are increasing 245 calories per day. Duplicated longer than a year that makes an aggregate of twenty five pounds! On the off chance that you had been any more astute you would have been 25 pounds more slender this year.

17. Caffeine association. All things considered, the vast majority are snared onto the caffeine of the bubbly beverages, so it will take you some effort to become accustomed to a no bubbly beverage diet.

18. Quit being blameworthy. Consider blame something that truly adds calories to your physical make-up.

19. Figure out how to ingrain trust in yourself. So consider the possibility that you had that additional glass of carbonated drink or that yummy looking truffle at the supper the previous evening. Offer yourself a reprieve! It doesn't mean anything. Proceed onward.

20. Each piece checks. With regards to weight reduction it's the easily overlooked details that issue.

Regardless of whether you dispose of a couple of calories for each day, these will duplicate to give you a general chop down of significantly more than you might suspect.

21. Keep an inspirational mentality about weight reduction. Value yourself at whatever point you can make any chop down or follow any eating regimen tip.

22. Try not to lose all sense of direction in calorie tallying. On the off chance that you are at a sentimental supper, drawing out a number cruncher to include supper calories may cause you to appear to be somewhat insane. Moreover, it basically sits idle.

23. Great food and awful food. The thought is to just separation all food into classes than knowing the

genuine tally. For instance natural products "low", sugar "high", yogurt "low" cream "high". Greek yogurt "low", mayonnaise "high".

24. Substitute fish and fish at every possible opportunity. At the point when you go out to eat, simply attempt to substitute with fish, similar to fish, lobster or shrimp at every possible opportunity. Fish is particularly powerful for ladies with PMS indications.

25. Diet breaks. You can make an incredible rundown of home prepared suppers and not have the option to do it ordinary. A partner may welcome you, a companion may draw you or perhaps you see a delicious feast in a magazine and you have to have some open air food. Well go, and be glad about it.

26. More on diet break. Consider a glitch in your eating routine program as a break, a get-away and not as something that will or has broken your weight reduction dream.

27. Forget about sugars. Cut down on the sugars however much as could reasonably be expected. At the point when you go out, request diet sweets. Rather than dessert attempt to build up the preference for solidified yogurt.

28. Diet plans. There are many eating regimen formula books accessible on the web and in book shops. On the off chance that you are an aficionado of cooking, at that point you can give them a shot at home.

29. Cheddar can be handled. In the

event that you are a major devotee of cheddar, at that point eliminating it may be somewhat unimaginable. So apply the stunts. For making nourishments like lasagna, you ought to select a more grounded cheddar. That way you get more flavor while the measure of cheddar, and consequently the measure of calories, is in reality less.

30. Try not to boycott dairy items. In this day of engineered nourishments, the couple of sound fixings left on our menu incorporates dairy items. In spite of the fact that dairy items may look loaded with calories, late investigations show that they really help in weight reduction! 31. Day by day dairy check. Obviously you can't go over the top. Downplay your day by day dairy check; say a glass of milk or a cut of cheddar.

32. Yogurt - I rest my case. On the off chance that I haven't focused on it enough, at that point I should state it again - yogurt is the new milk. Some yogurt has a larger number of proteins and nutrients than twofold the measure of milk.

33. Substitute plunges and dressings. You can likewise utilize Greek yogurt as a replacement for mayonnaise or cream based plunges and dressings.

34. Flame broiled is superior to singed. Albeit self-evident, this little stunt can assist you with losing a great deal of weight. Substitute barbecued, smoked or heated for singed at every possible opportunity. Regardless of whether its vegetables in Chinese or chicken in a burger.
35. Smoked is likewise superior to singed. Smoked fish is superior to

singed or even barbecued fish. Settle on these little solid decisions however much as could be expected and you will see those pounds dropping in any event, when you have been going out a ton.
36. A word about pizza. This is the most troublesome gorge to controls than some other maybe in light of the fact that a pizza truly isn't a wellbeing food. It's a little credulous to imagine that you will be cutting it totally, in light of the fact that you won't.

37. Pizza issues. Be that as it may, you do need to ensure you eat one not more than once per week. At the point when you do eat, you can settle on more advantageous decisions by requesting slight covering rather than profound dish.

38. Substitute low-fat or non-fat. Any place appropriate, utilize low fat milk,

cream, cheddar and even yogurt. You won't have the foggiest idea about the distinction when you eat yet your body will.

39. Cream is the genuine guilty party. It tends to be so difficult to abandon this on your treat. In any case, the best approach to deceive your body is to utilize it sparingly, so you don't wind up feeling denied.

40. Use whipped cream. One extraordinary tip is that one tablespoon of whipped cream conveys just around eight calories. So you can utilize it on a bowl of new foods grown from the ground away with it!

41. Try not to make each dairy non fat. Leave one dairy for every day or if nothing else each other day that isn't low fat or non fat. Particularly milk.

Nutritionists state this really helps weight reduction.

42. When eating out, request plate of mixed greens. This is an unquestionable requirement accomplish for your get-healthy plan. At the point when you consolidate a plate of mixed greens in your dinner, you get filled all the more rapidly and it leaves you no space for a greater amount of the principle course.

43. Consolidate action. No eating regimen can support you on the off chance that you are perched on your love seat and making yourself truly powerless and fat. It very well may be hard to fuse practice and your activity may not permit time for exercise center, however joining movement isn't just about causing yourself to go to the rec center for two days and afterward leaving it since something different came up.

44. Increasingly about action. Movement can be any action that causes you to feel better. I know this person who revealed to me how he got a kick out of the chance to help individuals conveying staple goods to their vehicles and utilizing this as an exercise! It caused him to feel better on the grounds that the individuals appeared to adore him and he was consuming calories simultaneously. Action can likewise be move exercises! Simply suppose you were get in shape while having the option to do salsa!

45. Margarine walk. In the event that you truly need that cream cheddar bagel, at that point you should stroll to go get it. Indeed, that is the new standard. Need that night doughnut? Stroll to get it. You have no clue about what number of calories you can

represent by doing this basic strolling custom.

46. Wholegrain versus white flour. The discussion has continued for quite a long time, and still remains constant. White flour identifies with weight gain, while wholegrain flour is natural and fills great need.

47. Everything isn't terrible. You should recall grains and starches are a piece of day by day diet and can't be prohibited from dinners, paying little mind to what those craze consumes less calories state.

48. Being tasteful makes a difference. It looks increasingly tasteful and trendy when you head off to some place and settle on every one of those sound food decisions - "Would i be able to have an entire wheat, cucumber

sandwich, and a glass of squeezed orange?" rather than "Gimme a mayonnaise sandwich and go substantial on the cheddar OK?"

49. End of the week clothing. Clearly what you wear on a lethargic end of the week chooses what you will eat on this apathetic end of the week as well. Nutritionists and dieticians affirm that wearing a perspiration shirt and flip lemon will keep you on the love seat with that potato chip pack, while enhancing formal wear will give you a sentiment of being cautious with what you eat.

50. Shop till you drop. This is just another approach to fuse a solid action. On the off chance that you like shopping, at that point simply shop and consume enough fat for a few days! Regardless of whether you

can't get, you should give things a shot or basically window shop.

51. At the point when you intend to go out. When arranging an excursion, attempt to program exercises that incorporate exercise as opposed to a basic eating of popcorn. Anything that incorporates in any event a touch of strolling would do.

52. Keep products of the soil convenient. You can't keep an eating regimen on the off chance that you don't have a loaded ice chest. Supposing that you prop up to the supermarket without fail, at that point you hazard losing the desire to keep at the natural product tidbit and you may enjoy something less interesting in transit. With a loaded cooler, at whatever point the inclination to eat strikes, you can just go get the organic

products or vegetables and begin filling yourself.

53. Try not to tune in to form models. Magazines sell stories, yet in addition the models and it is their business to cause it to appear as though everybody out there should resemble this. However, be canny and realize that it isn't accurate! Nobody you know is a runway model nor are you. So be sensible and love yourself the manner in which you are on the grounds that that is the thing that you are acceptable at.

54. Value yourself as far as possible. It is a basic enough activity, but we don't see numerous individuals attempting this.

55. Tip on appreciation. Regardless of whether you prevented yourself

from having a pizza today, or chatted on the telephone standing up, respect yourself for settling on the correct decision.

56. Make the most of your food. Try not to approach eating ceaselessly without even truly tasting the food. At the point when you fork something into your mouth, let your taste buds welcome the supper and appreciate it. Consider how exquisite that makes you look as well. Also, gradually you will end up eating increasingly slow. Recollect that food isn't tied in with filling, yet about getting a charge out of.

57. Figure out how to eat with chopsticks. Enjoy some tasteful food behavior. Be an epicurean and utilize chopsticks any place pertinent. It won't just top you off speedier,

however you will end up getting a charge out of the experience.

58. Add green tea and lemon to your food schedule. There are sufficient individuals out there requesting that you attempt green tea and lemon and revealing to you they aid fat consume.

There is proof to the opposite too, so you can't choose whether that is valid.

Yet, one thing is valid - green tea is an incredible method to give your body some recuperating elixir. In the case of nothing else, it will keep you off sweet beverages since it has a low measure of caffeine which can enable you to adapt. Regardless it is a lot more beneficial than a shaded harmful soft drink right?! Lemon may not really consume fat, however it helps digestion and gives you incredible skin.

59. Utilize nectar rather than sugar any place relevant. The achievability of non-sugar sugars is still getting looked at, so when remaining off sugar may look a bit of overwhelming, you can attempt to supplant nectar. Nectar is a natural and safe item and a few human advancements use it strictly for its gigantic medical advantages.

60. Think garments, not calories. There is no mischief in checking your gauging scale now and again, yet when you consider weight reduction, don't fixate on tallying calories and watching your gauging machine regular.

Now and again you will lose more and here and there less. Here and there your gauging machine won't give you anything besides your body will look all conditioned and extraordinary due to work out. So measure results by garments and how they fit, as opposed to gauging scales and calories.

Actually numerous individuals are fat and over weight on the grounds that all in all they are not content with themselves. Regardless of whether this is a direct result of the glossed over, fat loaded cheap food consumes less calories we have gained or whether it is basically in light of the fact that we have abandoned ourselves, we as a whole need assistance at some level.
The moment you figure out how to acknowledge yourself as what your identity is and understand a food gorge is only a passing extravagant, you will end up tolerating sound food and having the option to appreciate it as opposed to just approach eating it.

Concentrating on putting a specific sort of food aside isn't everybody's bit of cake and can really do you hurt. Most nutritionists will suggest a fair eating routine, which incorporates all nutrition types in the correct bits. Try not to take diet pills and patches except if you have talked about it with your primary care physician.

Recall one central principle: Do not think about an eating routine arrangement as being standard for a couple of days. These strategies referenced above are not an eating regimen program but rather an unpretentious, simple difference in way of life. You won't drop four sizes in a single month, yet you will lose a great deal of pounds over a more drawn out timeframe. This safe viable technique will ensure that rather than you putting on weight like
consistently and not having the option to fit into the pants you are wearing this year, you ought to have the option to fit into a years ago pants before the current year's over.

A few people have changed their whole schedules by utilizing these procedures and are not stressed any longer!

This is a sound way of life change which is more consistent and fruitful than an eating routine program. It works for as long as you can remember.
A snappy weight reduction diet plan is uncommon to discover. While there is no such a mind-bending concept as getting thinner short-term, there are diet designs that can really assist you with shedding a couple of pounds quick inside a week or as long as three weeks relying upon a couple of components about yourself. A great many people who are searching for a brisk method to decrease weight quick truly need an eating routine that works and is solid in any case. A speedy weight reduction diet program isn't fundamentally founded on

starvation so as to dispose of weight. Starving yourself to get in shape is unfortunate. Continue perusing to locate the best weight reduction diet I suggest.

Best Online Quick Weight Loss Diet Program
Fat Loss 4 Idiots: This is one of the most famous downloaded diet program on the web. In the previous not many years, fat misfortune 4 numbskulls has been ruling on line in the weight reduction industry as extraordinary compared to other eating regimen plans for quick weight reduction. Numerous individuals have utilized this program and shed pounds and that is presumably one reason why fat misfortune 4 blockheads is famous. So what is this program about? Fat misfortune 4 nitwits depends on an idea of "Calorie

Shifting" rather that eating low carb, low fat or low calories. Calorie moving isn't tied in with starving yourself either. It intends to shift the proportion of nourishments like proteins, sugars and fats. Fat misfortune 4 numbskulls is definitely not a low calorie low carb diet yet it has a bit control area that controls the calories and carbs you devour so you simply don't eat anything you need in any case.

The principle explanations behind moving calories is to permit digestion to acclimate to your eating routine and furthermore not to get exhausted eating same dinners constantly. At the point when you utilize the moving calorie strategy, for example, the one found in this fast weight reduction diet program, you accelerate your digestion and keep it high constantly. The final products will be consuming a bigger number of calories than you might suspect. Fat misfortune 4 morons likewise has an on line feast generator which lets you select the nourishments you like from the rundown that has a wide assortment of solid food sources. This quick weight reduction online program is easy to follow and the methods that are illustrated inside the program itself are demonstrated to work. Fat misfortune 4 numbskulls is commendable difficult and my solitary analysis is that it doesn't accentuate working out. This program can assist you with getting more fit quick yet it would be vastly improved whenever joined with a fundamental work out regime.

Fat misfortune 4 Idiots asserts that you can shed 9 pounds in 11 days which can be ridiculous to a great many people.

Strip That Fat Diet Plan: This is another get-healthy plan that I will just

say it unravels what fat misfortune for boneheads hasn't understood.
Tune in the event that you have been starving yourself for shedding pounds, With this program, you can eat as much solid nourishments from it's menu as you need while you are getting thinner.
On the off chance that you fall under the class of those that accept that the following quick weight reduction trend would work for them, at that point I surmise you ought to have a total reevaluate. To be open, this fast in and out eating regimens have nothing to offer with the exception of the loss of water weight and shockingly - bulk.

I don't get this' meaning? It implies that accomplishing a genuine weight reduction really includes a drawn out pledge to rebuilding one's way of life from beginning to end, in particular when it identifies with one's eating routine and exercise. Despite the fact that, there exist a couple of circumstances when maybe a moment weight reduction would be acceptable. Albeit quick weight reduction strategies do come convenient in certain circumstances, yet for a maintainable outcomes, you have to show responsibility and excitement towards rethinking your way of life that predominantly focuses on your eating regimen and exercise. Other quick weight decreasing strategies just outcome in water weight reduction or bulk misfortune. A certifiable weight reduction requires time, tolerance and responsibility. In any case, in certain circumstances, you can utilize these quick weight reduction designs that can come convenient.

Can hardly wait? Need Fast Results?

Is it true that you are only a couple of additional pounds a long way from arriving at your optimal weight? Would you like to dispose of these couple of additional pounds? Furthermore, would you truly like to dispose of these additional pounds inside two or three weeks? In the event that your answer is truly, at that point the main answer for you is to show solid resolve and begin dealing with your quick weight reduction plan now.

One of the most significant pieces of any weight reduction strategy is over the top drinking of water. Regardless of whether you are utilizing shorter and impermanent weight diminishing plans or long haul and lasting weight lessening plans, drinking over the top measures of water is an absolute necessity in each weight decreasing arrangement.

Drinking more water brings about flushing progressively fat; henceforth hydrating your body. Another favorable position of drinking more water is the way that by doing this, you will eat less in light of the fact that your stomach would be as of now loaded up with water. So it is constantly prescribed to drink a glass of water before your beginning your feast, along these lines, you will eat less.

Eating less is actually a troublesome errand if your stomach is unfilled and you have your preferred supper before you. Be that as it may, regardless of whether you have your preferred dinner before you however you have had enough water before it, at that point you would eat not as much as what you would have eaten on the off chance that you hadn't had enough water before it.

In a quick weight reduction strategy, you will be required to remove the admission of sweet beverages, likewise called as bubbly beverages. You can substitute bubbly beverages with skimmed milk or zero calorie drinks. On the off chance that you can proceed with this, it will ensure weight reduction of roughly 15 pounds in a year. However, this can't be accomplished in the event that you haven't cut off fat and starches from your every day diet.

Here are some progressively helpful thoughts.

In the event that you get any club together with the expectation of diminishing load by not utilizing quick weight losing techniques then you require extremely solid self control since it will require some investment. In the event that you objective is to lessen weight, at that point you should show solid self control. Be that as it may, as referenced prior, there are times when a quick weight reduction strategy can really support you

You can utilize these strategies during your battle for lessening weight utilizing customary eating routine and exercise techniques; making quick weight reduction as an auxiliary strategy joined by the essential eating regimen and exercise.

The Hidden Secret of Negative-Calorie Foods - One mystery to shedding that abundance pounds is that drilled by most quick weight reduction specialists which is the taking-in of negative calorie nourishments instead of fatty nourishments. One needs to remember that each food contains calories yet for a specific food to pick up that negative calorie mark, the body would need to consume more vitality in processing it for additional assimilation.

www.ingramcontent.com/pod-product-compliance
Lightning Source LLC
Chambersburg PA
CBHW08083716726
47999CB00009B/2919